This book
belongs to...

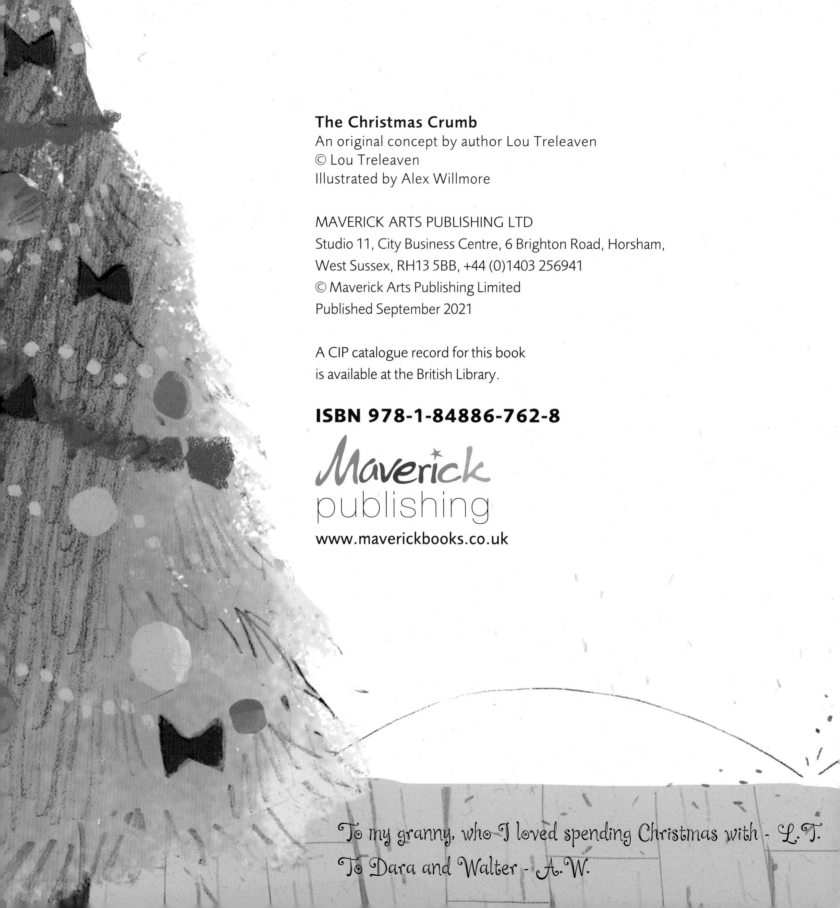

The Christmas Crumb
An original concept by author Lou Treleaven
© Lou Treleaven
Illustrated by Alex Willmore

MAVERICK ARTS PUBLISHING LTD
Studio 11, City Business Centre, 6 Brighton Road, Horsham,
West Sussex, RH13 5BB, +44 (0)1403 256941
© Maverick Arts Publishing Limited
Published September 2021

A CIP catalogue record for this book
is available at the British Library.

ISBN 978-1-84886-762-8

Maverick
publishing
www.maverickbooks.co.uk

To my granny, who I loved spending Christmas with - L.T.

To Dara and Walter - A.W.

The Christmas CRUMB

Written by Lou Treleaven

Illustrated by Alex Willmore

Way up in the clouds, where the air is much thinner,

A giant royal family ate Christmas dinner.

With turkey and sausages large as a limb

And gravy so deep you could get in and swim.

And after they'd eaten a meal that was **flawless,**

A pudding arrived that was **simply enormous!**

They gobbled and gorged till they couldn't eat more.

Then a piece crumbled off and rolled out of the door.

"Oops!" cried the giant princess. "Sorry, Mum!"

"Don't worry, my poppet, it's only a crumb.

So itsy, so bitsy, it's not worth the fussing.

It's quite unimportant – it really is nothing."

In a tumbledown cottage, Pip sat with his mother.

They didn't have much, but they did have each other.

When all of a sudden the doorframe gave way
And a giant pud flattened the Christmas display.

"This prize Christmas Pudding's as big as my head!

Forget our thin gruel, we can eat this instead!"

Pip took up a spoon and
devoured his share.

But a small piece broke off and rolled under the chair.

Pip searched for the morsel. "I've dropped a bit, Mum."

"Don't worry, my dearest, it's only a crumb.
So dinky, so diddy, it's not worth the fussing.
It's inconsequential – it really is nothing."

Down in a mouse hole, a dozen mice pups

Were getting quite desperate for food to turn up.

They'd picked the wrong cottage to live in, for sure.

Then Father Mouse rolled a great feast through the door.

"You've saved us!" cried Mother as all the pups squeaked.

"This vast Christmas Pudding will feed us for weeks."

They scurried all over it, ready to scoff.

But the tiniest piece came apart and rolled off...

The baby mice chirruped, "We've missed a bit, Mum."

"Don't worry, my treasures, it's only a crumb.

So teeny, so tiny, it's not worth the fussing.

It's hardly much more than a dot – really nothing."

Outside in the garden, some ants in a line

Were putting down leaf cuttings, ready to dine,

When all of a sudden a gigantic crumb

Rolled onto their table, and dinner was done!

"I've heard of these **puddings**," said one ant, impressed,

"But this one is almost as big as our nest!

We'll make it through winter. We're going to survive!

This huge Christmas Pudding has just saved our lives."

But one ant stood back and was making a face.

"I hope you don't think that I speak out of place.

I can't stand Christmas Pudding. It just isn't me."

And he passed his share down to an overjoyed flea.

So remember this Christmas

that what might seem small

And mean nothing to you,

to another means all.